WHAT GRANDPAS DO BEST

Grandpas can play hide-and-seek,

make you a hat,

and take you for a walk.

Grandpas can paint with you,

show you their photographs,

and teach you how to dance.

Grandpas can take you on a picnic,

show you some magic tricks,

and help you fly a kite.

Grandpas can take you to the beach,

help you build a sand castle,

and take a nap with you.

Grandpas can play games with you,

give you a bath,

and sing you a lullaby.

But best of all,
grandpas can give you
lots and lots of love.

But best of all,
grandmas can give you
lots and lots of love.

and sing you a lullaby.

give you a bath,

Grandmas can play games with you,

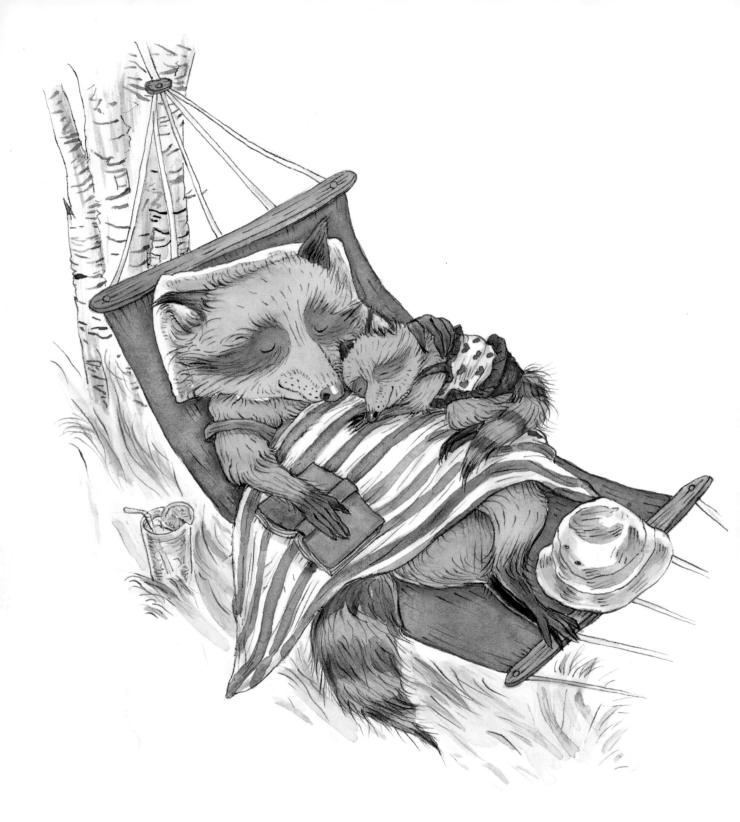

and take a nap with you.

help you build a sand castle,

Grandmas can take you to the beach,

and help you fly a kite.

show you some magic tricks,

Grandmas can take you on a picnic,

and teach you how to dance.

show you their photographs,

Grandmas can paint with you,

and take you for a walk.

make you a hat,

Grandmas can play hide-and-seek,

WHAT
GRANDMAS
DO BEST

BY **Laura Numeroff**

ILLUSTRATED BY **Lynn Munsinger**

SIMON & SCHUSTER BOOKS FOR YOUNG READERS

NEW YORK   LONDON   TORONTO   SYDNEY   SINGAPORE